Daniel Boone

Daniel Boone

Academic Industries, Inc.
West Haven, Connecticut 06516

ISBN 0-88301-777-6

Published by
Academic Industries, Inc.
The Academic Building
Saw Mill Road
West Haven, Connecticut 06516

Printed in the United States of America

Daniel Boone

Contents

Daniel Boone lived all his life in Indian country. Once, when there were Indians all around him, he escaped by jumping from a cliff.

Daniel was caught by the Indians many times. He also escaped many times. He was able to stay alive because he knew the ways of the woods.

The Pioneer

When Daniel was three years old, his family moved to a faraway place that was to become Reading, Pennsylvania.

Where will our new home be?

This looks like a good spot right here!

Daniel's father and the older boys went to work cutting down trees.

They built a log house in the small clearing they had made.

Then they plowed the ground and planted a crop.

Father Boone also taught his sons everything he knew about the woods.

You must learn to see everything in the woods and to hear every sound.

Most Indians around here are peaceful. But in case a brave is on the warpath, you must see him first, and slip away like a shadow!

And you must walk softly so that you don't make any noise.

It is your job to bring the cows home at night. You must notice the sun or the moon, the way the wind blows,—everything. Then you can find your way home again.

These lessons were fun. But they were also a matter of life and death. Daniel learned them well.

As soon as he could hold a gun, Daniel was taught to shoot.

Steady . . . line up your sights.

Then he learned to hunt.

You got him!

Never waste a shot, Daniel. There's plenty of game, but you must be careful not to run out of gunpowder.

Daniel loved being in the woods. He soon knew more about them than anyone else.

Sometimes he hunted and camped with friendly Indian boys.

You come see Indian village?

I'd like that!

Women do camp work. Indian braves track animals, hunt, fish, fight!

I wish I were an Indian! I think I'd make a good one.

Daniel also listened to the white men tell about Indian fights and Indian tricks they had seen.

Daniel kept quiet, but he did not agree.

There's one thing for sure—you can't trust an Indian. They don't think the way we do!

I *can* think like an Indian. Except for my color, I'm more like an Indian than a white boy!

16

When Daniel was fifteen, his father decided to move to a new place.

Get ready—we're moving on! This farm land is worn out, and there are too many people coming in.

Where are we going?

Southwest, where there's rich land for sale and lots of game to hunt.

More game, new country to explore, and fewer people! That's great!

So the Boone family packed up their wagon and began their long journey. They stopped at last in the Yadkin valley in North Carolina.

Plenty of good land, and plenty of grass for the cows.

Someday I'll see what lies west, over the mountains.

Once again they had the hard job of clearing land and building a cabin.

Somebody has to get us meat, and you're worth any two of us as a hunter! Go ahead, Daniel!

Sure!

POCKET BIOGRAPHIES

Daniel brought back rabbits and turkeys.

Often he shot a deer . . .

. . . and sometimes even a bear.

The skin will make a fine, warm cover!

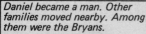

Daniel became a man. Other families moved nearby. Among them were the Bryans.

Daniel, this is our new neighbor, Rebecca Bryan.

Soon there was a wedding.

Do you, Daniel, take this woman, Rebecca. . . .

The neighbors came from many miles around to join the wedding party.

Hunting
and
Trapping
in Kentucky

21

In 1769 Boone, Finley, and six strong men went to see the new land.

We'll look it over and see if it's a good place to live.

We'll get along fine here. The boys are old enough to help with the work.

When the men left, they expected good weather. Instead, it rained for many days.

At night they slept in a lean-to, a kind of tent. The lean-to kept them warm and dry, and hid their fire from the Indians.

Seven weeks later they made their way up the last steep hill to Cumberland Gap.

There it is, Daniel— Kentucky!

It's beautiful, John, just as you said.

They hurried down to take a closer look at it.

I've never seen so many wild turkeys in my life!

There were great herds of deer.

There were almost as many bears.

They were surprised most of all by the large number of buffalo.

There must be more buffalo here than cattle back home!

The men built a small cabin on a river. Then they went to look around and to hunt.

There's game and rich land everywhere. But it takes other things to make a good place for a settlement.

You need high ground and a forest that isn't too thick . . . maple trees nearby . . . salt licks . . . and good water.

They had seen no Indians. Then, on December 22, Daniel was hunting with John Stuart. Suddenly, they found Indians on all sides.

Don't let them know you're afraid. It's the best way.

The Indians took Boone and Stuart with them.

Let them think we're glad to go with them, and that we want to join their tribe.

But don't ever try to escape and fail! Then they'll kill you for sure!

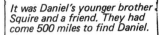

It was Daniel's younger brother Squire and a friend. They had come 500 miles to find Daniel.

Well, we've caught up with you at last. We have fresh supplies and ammunition for you.

Thanks! You're just in time!

Soon the men began hunting again. One night Stuart did not return. The next day, Daniel searched the forest for him.

I found no sign of Stuart!

Let's get away from here! The Indians will find us if we stay!

We can't quit now. This is our chance to be rich.

We'll be very careful!

Stay if you like! I'm going home!

So Neeley left for home—and was never seen again. The Boones hunted and trapped, and did their best to stay away from the Indians. In the spring they had many furs.

They decided that Squire would go home, sell the furs, and return with more bullets and supplies.

I figure I can be back in two months. Take care of yourself!

You take care! My rifle and I will get along fine!

While he was alone, Daniel saw most of Kentucky. What he learned in his travels would be very useful later.

Squire came back in July. He had sold the furs, paid the money they owed, and bought supplies.

He and Daniel did more hunting and trapping and then went home.

It's hard to believe that these are the little fellows I left behind!

You've been gone a good while, Daniel!

Two years later, Daniel decided to move to Kentucky. Six other families went with the Boones.

It's a good, strong group. We have everything we need to settle in Kentucky.

The trip was a rough and slow one, but at last they camped near Cumberland Gap.

We'll wait here for the forty men who are coming to join us with Captain Russell.

James, you ride back to Russell's cabin and help bring the supplies he promised.

Yes, Father!

28

Across
Cumberland
Gap

On the way back from Russell's cabin, James Boone and his men camped overnight. An Indian war party surprised them at daybreak.

All were killed except two of Russell's men.

The Boones and their friends were sad. Many were frightened.

It's a warning! The Indians want no settlements in Kentucky!

How can forty of us fight thousands of Indians?

We're going back!

Maybe this is not the time. But I'll build a place near here and wait.

The Boones and a few other families decided to stay in a nearby valley.

But Daniel was not there long. Lord Dunmore, the British governor of Virginia, sent for them.

I have sent men into Kentucky to see the land. But the Indians have attacked them all.

You are the only one who might reach my men and lead them to safety.

I'll go at once!

He had to walk 800 miles in two months. But Daniel led the men out.

31

Meanwhile, many Indians were making war on the people of Virginia. Finally, however, they were defeated by Dunmore's army.

This gave ideas to a man named Henderson.

Only the Cherokees still want Kentucky. I'll buy it, then sell it to white men. I'll give you 3,000 acres to help me.

I'll get the Cherokees together for a meeting.

Fine! Then take thirty men and cut a road over the mountains.

The Indians agreed to sell Kentucky to Henderson. Daniel began clearing a road across Cumberland Gap.

Knowing the country, Daniel found a good place for his road. People would come to know it as the Wilderness Road. In ten weeks he reached the spot he had chosen for their town.

This is the Kentucky River! I'll send word to Henderson to bring his people here.

Later, the town was named Boonesborough in Daniel's honor.

Daniel returned to Boonesborough in September with Rebecca and Jemima, one of his daughters.

This is the Kentucky River. You are the first white women to see it!

It's beautiful, Daniel!

Nearly a year passed. The Boones were happy. Then one summer day, Jemima and two friends went for a canoe ride. The boat struck some sand and stopped.

We're stuck! Push us off!

I don't want to get my feet wet!

All at once, Indians jumped from the bushes.

No! Stop!

Let us go!

But the Indians grabbed the girls and took them away.

You go with us—and be quiet!

All right.

At sunset the girls were missed. Daniel found their empty canoe.

Indians! They'll head north. We'll follow them.

A broken twig! A scrap of cloth! The girls have tried to leave signs for us!

The men hurried on. Daniel took short-cuts. They went forty miles.

There they are! But be careful! When we surprise them, they will try to kill the girls!

Daniel told the men where to shoot. They crept forward without a sound and took aim.

Ready . . . fire!

It's Father!

The Indians who were not killed ran away. The men took the happy girls back home.

Soon the first wedding in Kentucky took place. Betsy Callaway married one of the young men who had saved her from the Indians.

Before long, Jemima Boone and Frances Callaway also married two young men from Boonesborough.

But Indian trouble was getting worse.

The Shawnees attacked our forts!

The British are giving them weapons to drive us out of Kentucky!

Many frightened families moved back east again.

Only twenty-two guns left to defend Boonesborough!

And not more than a hundred in all of Kentucky!

There was not much food left. And there was no salt to keep meat from spoiling. So Daniel led a party of men to find salt.

They had to boil hundreds of gallons of salt water to get salt. And there was another problem.

We're out of meat, Daniel.

I'll go hunting.

Permanent Settlements At Last

While he was hunting, Daniel was caught by Indians.

There are too many of them!

There was no chance of escape. Daniel was taken to the Indian chief, Blackfoot.

I am happy to see my old friend, the great Chief Blackfoot.

And I, to greet the great white chief, Boone! Welcome!

Blackfoot had many men with him. They were on their way to Boonesborough. And Boonesborough was very weak! Daniel knew he must think of a way to save the fort.

Don't go now. They are too strong for your small war party!

We are tired of fighting. At the right time, we will gladly leave our town.

Wait until spring! Then my people will be happy to move north with you.

So instead of attacking the fort, the Indians went back north to their villages, taking Daniel with them.

Boone, I will make you my son!

You do me a great honor.

Daniel was given the Indian name of Big Turtle.

But still he found no chances to escape. And in the spring a big war party made ready to go to Boonesborough.

Five hundred Indians to attack Boonesborough! I must escape and give some warning!

Later, when he was out hunting, Daniel ran away. The fastest and best Indians chased him. He ran 125 miles in five days to reach the fort.

Daniel! You're safe!

Send some men for help! Make the walls stronger! Bring in plenty of food and water! Indians are coming to attack us!

Soon the Indians appeared.

We have thirty men. Blackfoot has nearly five hundred. We must hold them off as long as we can and wait for help.

For days Daniel kept the Indians away, talking with Blackfoot. But at last the talking ended.

Here they come! We'll defend the fort as long as there is a man left alive!

From behind every tree and bush the Indians fired at the fort.

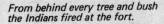

The women and children made bullets and loaded guns.

Make every shot count, men!

The battle went on for eight days. There was no time to rest. Water ran low, and no help came.

Then the Indians shot blazing arrows onto the dry roofs. They also built fires near the walls of the fort.

Finally, there was no more water.

But suddenly came a clap of thunder, and rain poured down, putting out the fires.

It's a miracle!

The next morning the Indians were gone. The fort was saved. There would be more battles with the Indians, but from that day on, white people were in Kentucky to stay.

Soon others came by the thousands. They all wanted land. One morning the sheriff came to take Daniel's farm away from him.

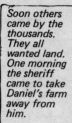

I'm sorry, Daniel! But some people say you don't own your farm.

I've opened up miles and miles of land to these people and fought off Indians. Now they want to take away my small part of it?

So Daniel lost his farm. It was not until many years later that the United States government voted to give him 1,000 acres.

There are too many people and towns here! It's time we moved along.

They went west to Missouri. At that time it belonged to Spain, and people knew all about Daniel Boone there.

Señor Boone, it is an honor to have you here! We will give you 1,000 acres of land.

He accepted their offer gladly.

Daniel Boone lived to be eighty-six years old. People never stopped coming to visit him to hear his stories.

Tell us one of your Indian stories, Mr. Boone!

I will. But first I'll tell you about the lands to the west. There are so many places still left to explore!

THE END

Do you remember?

When he was three years old, Daniel Boone's father moved to a settlement that became:

a. New York.   b. Vermont.   c. Pennsylvania.

Daniel Boone explored the land and cut a trail to Cumberland Gap, opening up the area that became:

a. Ohio.   b. Kentucky.   c. Kansas.

Daniel was taken into an Indian tribe as Chief Blackfoot's son. He was given the name of:

a. Flying Dove.　　　b. Big Turtle.　　　c. Hunting Owl.

Daniel warned the settlers that 500 Indian braves would attack:

a. Boonesborough.　　　b. New York.　　　c. Santa Fe.

44

Quiz
Yourself

(Answers at end of section)

Words to know

game	wild animals, birds, or fish hunted or caught
journey	travel from one place to another
settlement	a group of buildings and the people who live in them
supplies	the food and other things necessary for a settlement to exist
track	follow by means of footprints, smell, or any mark left by something that has passed by

Can you use them?

Using the words above, complete the following sentences.

1. The _____ from Virginia to Kentucky took several weeks in Daniel Boone's time.

2. The pioneers often had problems getting _____ to their new settlements.

3. Daniel Boone was a good hunter because he knew how to _____ animals.

4. Birds, fish, and land animals which are used for food are called _____ .

5. The _____ in which Boone lived was on high ground near the river.

POCKET BIOGRAPHIES

Using pictures

In reading illustrated
stories, you will find it helpful
to "read" the pictures as well
as the words. Look at this pic-
ture. It shows us how pioneers
built their cabins. Whole tree
trunks were used as building
materials. Look carefully at
the other pictures as you read
and you will learn more about
how things were done in pio-
neer days.

While you are reading

Even though Daniel Boone understood the Indians and was sometimes their friend, he often had problems with them. While you are
reading, make a list of the times
Daniel Boone had problems with
the Indians.

_____

_____

_____

_____

_____

How well did you read?

When you have finished reading, answer the following questions.

1. What things did Daniel's father teach him that helped him get along in the woods?

   (Check the correct *answers.*)

   _____ a. to know where water could be found

   _____ b. to listen to every sound

   _____ c. to walk softly and make no noise

   _____ d. to watch the sun and moon so as not to become lost

   _____ e. to find the good salt licks

   _____ f. to see an Indian before he saw you

2. Listed below are the things settlers had to do in order to build a new settlement. Number them in the order they were done by writing 1 in front of the first thing they had to do, 2 in front of the next, and so on.

   _____ a. Plant crops for food.

   _____ b. Build a fort for protection.

   _____ c. Find high ground close to a forest, water, and trees.

   _____ d. Clear the land of trees.

3. What was the miracle that saved Boonesborough from Indian attack?

    (Check the correct answer.)

    _____ a.   The settlers were able to kill all the Indians.

    _____ b.   A thunder-storm put out the fires started by the Indians' arrows.

    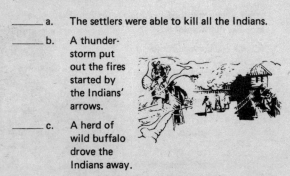

    _____ c.   A herd of wild buffalo drove the Indians away.

    _____ d.   The soldiers arrived just in time.

4. Why did Daniel Boone and his family keep moving west?

    (Check the correct answer.)

    _____ a.   They wanted more game, country to explore, and fewer neighbors.

    _____ b.   The sheriff was after them.

    _____ c.   The government kept sending Daniel to explore new lands.

    _____ d.   Daniel's settlements kept being destroyed by Indians.

5. Why was Daniel Boone so disappointed when the sheriff took his land away?

   (Check the correct answer.)

_____ a. He had spent all his money buying the land.

_____ b. The president had given him this land for his years of service to the country.

_____ c. The land had been in his family for generations.

_____ d. He had opened miles of this land for settlers and had fought off the Indians.

Using what you've read

When Daniel Boone was a young man, he said, "Except for my color, I'm more like an Indian than a white boy." From what you have read about Daniel Boone, what do you think he meant by this? In a short paragraph, explain why Daniel Boone was more like an Indian than a white boy.

DANIEL BOONE

Can you use them?

1. journey
2. supplies
5. settlement
3. track
4. game

How well did you read?

1. b, c, d, f
2. a-4, b-3, c-1, d-2
5. d
3. b
4. a

NOTES

NOTES

NOTES

NOTES

COMPLETE LIST OF POCKET CLASSICS AVAILABLE

CLASSICS

C 1 Black Beauty
C 2 The Call of the Wild
C 3 Dr. Jekyll and Mr. Hyde
C 4 Dracula
C 5 Frankenstein
C 6 Huckleberry Finn
C 7 Moby Dick
C 8 The Red Badge of Courage
C 9 The Time Machine
C10 Tom Sawyer
C11 Treasure Island
C12 20,000 Leagues Under the Sea
C13 The Great Adventures of Sherlock Holmes
C14 Gulliver's Travels
C15 The Hunchback of Notre Dame
C16 The Invisible Man
C17 Journey to the Center of the Earth
C18 Kidnapped
C19 The Mysterious Island
C20 The Scarlet Letter
C21 The Story of My Life
C22 A Tale of Two Cities
C23 The Three Musketeers
C24 The War of the Worlds
C25 Around the World in Eighty Days
C26 Captains Courageous
C27 A Connecticut Yankee in King Arthur's Court
C28 The Hound of the Baskervilles
C29 The House of the Seven Gables
C30 Jane Eyre

C31 The Last of the Mohicans
C32 The Best of O. Henry
C33 The Best of Poe
C34 Two Years Before the Mast
C35 White Fang
C36 Wuthering Heights
C37 Ben Hur
C38 A Christmas Carol
C39 The Food of the Gods
C40 Ivanhoe
C41 The Man in the Iron Mask
C42 The Prince and the Pauper
C43 The Prisoner of Zenda
C44 The Return of the Native
C45 Robinson Crusoe
C46 The Scarlet Pimpernel
C47 The Sea Wolf
C48 The Swiss Family Robinson
C49 Billy Budd
C50 Crime and Punishment
C51 Don Quixote
C52 Great Expectations
C53 Heidi
C54 The Illiad
C55 Lord Jim
C56 The Mutiny on Board H.M.S. Bounty
C57 The Odyssey
C58 Oliver Twist
C59 Pride and Prejudice
C60 The Turn of the Screw